THE HARDY BOYS

#9

UNDERCOVER BROTHERS™

To Die Or Not To Die?

SCOTT LOBDELL • Writer
PAULO HENRIQUE • Artist
Based on the series by
FRANKLIN W. DIXON

New York

J-GN
HARDY BOYS
367-4028

To Die Or Not To Die?
SCOTT LOBDELL — Writer
PAULO HENRIQUE — Artist
MARK LERER — Letterer
LAURIE E. SMITH — Colorist
JIM SALICRUP — Editor-in-Chief

ISBN 10: 1-59707-062-9 paperback edition
ISBN 13: 978-1-59707-062-1 paperback edition
ISBN 10: 1-59707-063-7 hardcover edition
ISBN 13: 978-1-59707-063-8 hardcover edition

Printed in China

10   9   8   7   6   5   4   3   2   1

CHAPTER ONE:
"A HORROR IN ONE!"

CHAPTER THREE: "EXIT STAGE LEFT-- FOREVER!"

THAT STAGE LIGHT?!

SMASH!

CHAPTER FOUR:
"TAKING THE SHOW
ON THE ROAD!"

CHAPTER SIX: "WALK... DON'T RUN!"

I THOUGHT I SAW JOELLE SLEEPWALKING!

BUT IF SHE MISSTEPS, SHE'LL BE KILLED!

CHAPTER SEVEN: "LIGHT OF THE WORLD!"

K-KRASH!

CHAPTER ONE:
"THE HIGHER THEY ARE...
THE FARTHER THEY FALL!"

BUT IF THINGS DON'T TURN AROUND SOON...

...I'M GOING TO BE LITTLE MORE THAN A STAIN 10,000 FEET FROM NOW!

I'VE BEEN GETTING AWAY WITH MY CON FOR MONTHS.

YOU AND YOUR BROTHER HAVE COST ME THOUSANDS!

THAT'S NOT EVEN COUNTING THE LENGTHY PRISON TERM WHEN YOU'RE FINALLY CONVICTED.

Don't miss THE HARDY BOYS Graphic Novel # 10 – "A Hardy's Day Night"

THE HARDY BOYS

UNDERCOVER BROTHERS™

ATAC BRIEFING FOR AGENTS FRANK AND JOE HARDY

#13: THE MUMMY'S CURSE
Available December 2006

MISSION:

A man has been murdered, possibly over a map to a precious golden mummy. Are there other treasure-hunters trying to find the location of the tomb? Could there be a curse surrounding the ancient mummy and his treasure?

LOCATION:

Cairo, Egypt, and the surrounding area.

SUSPECTS:

Several people on an expedition are suspects. you have to find them before they find the mummy . . . and his treasure!

THIS MISSION REQUIRES YOUR IMMEDIATE ATTENTION. PICK UP A COPY OF *THE MUMMY'S CURSE* AND GET ON THE CASE!

Have you read Frank and Joe's latest stories of crime, danger, mystery, and death-defying stunts?

TOP TEN WAYS TO DIE

MARTIAL LAW

BLOWN AWAY

HURRICANE JOE

TROUBLE IN PARADISE

Visit www.SimonSaysSleuth.com for more Hardy Boys adventures.

 ALADDIN PAPERBACKS • SIMON & SCHUSTER CHILDREN'S PUBLISHING

The Hardy Boys © Simon & Schuster, Inc.

WATCH OUT FOR PAPERCUT₂

Papercutz Editor-in-Chief Jim Salicrup here with something really important to say to you before we kick off this edition of the Papercutz back-pages: **Thank you!**

Thank you for picking up this Papercutz book. Whether this is your very first Papercutz graphic novel or your second, third, fourth, or sixteenth—we greatly appreciate it. We work around the clock to make each and every one of our books the very best we possibly can, so that you can get the absolute maximum amount of enjoyment from each and every page. But it's all for nothing without you!

And thanks to you, Papercutz has become quite a success story. We suspect that's because instead of offering more of the same types of comics that were already being published, Papercutz is devoted to bringing our own brand of fun and excitement to the world of graphic novels.

Thanks to you also for telling us what you like and don't like about Papercutz. That's been a huge help to us in choosing our new, upcoming Papercutz titles. By revealing how much you enjoy the humor in our mystery and adventure titles, such as The Hardy Boys, Nancy Drew, and Totally Spies, we knew our new titles had to be just as much fun. We'll soon be adding a horror anthology to our line-up. And it'll have that Papercutz sense of humor. The new title is revealed on the next few pages, but there's a mighty big clue on this page!

EDITOR-IN-CHIEF

THE CRYPT-KEEPER

But before you get to the big announcement, on behalf of all the Papercutz writers and artists, allow me to thank you one more time for giving us the opportunity to do what we love— create the very best graphic novels we can for you!

Thanks,

Jim

Caricature of Jim drawn by Steve Brodner at the MoCCA Art Fest. The Crypt-Keeper is © 2007 William M. Gaines, Agent, Inc.

PAPERCUTZ™

presents:
The Return of
TALES FROM THE CRYPT®

It's one of the biggest surprises in the world of comics and graphic novel publishing! Shortly before the 2007 New York Comic Con, we announced that Papercutz would be publishing all-new TALES FROM THE CRYPT comics. After more than 50 years, EC Comics' legendary flagship title returns with all-new TALES FROM THE CRYPT, narrated by the original Crypt-Keeper, Old Witch, and Vault Keeper. Each issue will feature two 20-page tales of terror in the EC tradition!

Reactions ranged from excitement— from fans thrilled to see the most famous horror comicbook ever return after over fifty years, to shock—that it was to be coming from a publisher primarily known for its graphic novels such as Nancy Drew and The Hardy Boys which contain material suitable for all-ages, as the HBO series certainly contained a fair amount of adult content.

"People forget that the original TALES FROM THE CRYPT comicbook, published by the legendary EC Comics back in the 50s, was also intended for all-ages, and its primary readership was young boys," Papercutz Editor-in-Chief Jim Salicrup is quick to point out. But that may be exactly what fans find so controversial. The original TALES FROM THE CRYPT comics, featuring stories dreamed up by EC publisher William M. Gaines and his editor Al Feldstein, and drawn by Feldstein, as well as Graham Ingles, Jack Davis, Jack Kamen, Joe Orlando, Wally Wood, Harvey Kurtzman, Bill Elder, Reed Crandall, Johnny Craig, Al Williamson, George Evans, and colored by Marie Severin, started a horror comics craze that soon drew the attention of psychiatrist Dr. Frederick Wertham.

Wertham reacted to the popularity of horror comics with children by writing a book called "Seduction of the Innocent," which maintained that comics led to juvenile delinquency and even worse behavior. Parents were understandably alarmed, and soon the Senate Subcommittee to Investigate Juvenile Delinquency was taking a hard look at comicbooks. EC Comics publisher Bill Gaines spoke before the Subcommittee, but was unable to convince them that his comics were entertaining stories told in good taste. Ultimately, comicbook publishers adversely affected by the negative publicity created the Comics Magazine Association of America which would review comics and award a seal of approval to assure parents that the comic's contents were safe, wholesome entertainment.

Unfortunately, it was too late for many publishers, as the negative publicity had so hurt sales of comics that many comicbook companies went out of business. EC Comics, tried to hang in there, but despite canceling their horror comics, and creating new titles such as "Valor" and "Psychoanalysis," only MAD comics, in a new magazine format, survived.

The question is, was TALES FROM CRYPT really all that bad? "Of course not!" Salicrup insists. "Ironically, many of the original stories would be approved by today's revised Comics Code, but sure, there were some stories that still wouldn't get by. The point here is that the stories that Papercutz will be creating will be aimed at readers age 10 and up. Instead of excessive blood and gore, we'll be sticking to the TALES FROM THE CRYPT tradition of stories filled with interesting characters, lots of dark humor, and of course, the trademarked EC "shock" endings!" The first TALES FROM THE CRYPT comic from Papercutz, which will be on sale in comics shops in June, features:

•"Body of Work," by horror author Marc Bilgrey (H.P. Lovecraft's Magazine of Horror, "And Don't Forget to Rescue the Princess") and Mr. Exes (Abra Cadaver). The story reveals how two nosy and somewhat murderous neighbors discover the shocking inspiration for Jack Kroll's creepy "outsider" artwork.

• "For Serious Collectors Only," by Rob Vollmar (Bluesman) and Tim Smith III (Teen Titans Go!). This tale explores how far Thomas Donalley— a middle-aged action-figure collector who lives in his mom's basement— will go for an ultra-rare Japanese figure.

•Introductory pages featuring the GhouLunatics are written by editor Jim Salicrup and drawn by artist Rick Parker (Beavis and Butt-Head).

• Cover by award-winning artist Kyle Baker (Nat Turner, Plastic Man, Why I Hate Saturn).

Future issues will include stories by Fred Van Lente (Marvel Adventures), Xeric Grant winner Neil Kleid, Stefan Petrucha (The Shadow of Frankenstein, NANCY DREW), Don McGregor (ZORRO), Sho Murase (NANCY DREW), and other great talents. Each bi-monthly issue is 48 full-color pages for an affordable $3.95. Naturally, the comics will be collected in the usual 112 page, ($7.95 paperback; $12.95 hardcover) full-color digest format, with the first volume, TALES FROM THE CRYPT "Ghouls Gone Wild!" available in bookstores everywhere in time for Halloween.

When reached for comment, the Crypt-Keeper said, "It's good to be back, boils and ghouls—and it's about time! Ahahahah!"

The movie we've all been waiting for is almost here! To get a sneak peek, go online to: http://nancydrewmovie.warnerbros.com/ and watch the fun-filled, action-packed trailer plus a lot more. You'll get to see Nancy Drew in action, in lots of scenes from her soon to be released major motion picture!

The film follows Nancy (Emma Roberts) as she accompanies her father, Carson Drew (Tate Donovan), to Los Angeles on one of his business trips and stumbles across evidence about a long-unsolved crime involving the mysterious death of a beautiful movie star. Nancy's resourcefulness and personal responsibility are put to the test when she finds herself in the middle of the fast-living, self-indulgent world of Hollywood.

Nancy Drew (EMMA ROBERTS) in Warner Bros. Pictures' and Virtual Studios' teen drama action/adventure "Nancy Drew," distributed by Warner Bros. Pictures. Photo by Melinda Sue Gordon

Top to bottom: Ned (MAX THIERIOT), Nancy Drew (EMMA ROBERTS) and Corky (JOSH FLITTER) in Warner Bros. Pictures' and Virtual Studios' teen drama action/adventure "Nancy Drew," distributed by Warner Bros. Pictures. Photo by Melinda Sue Gordon

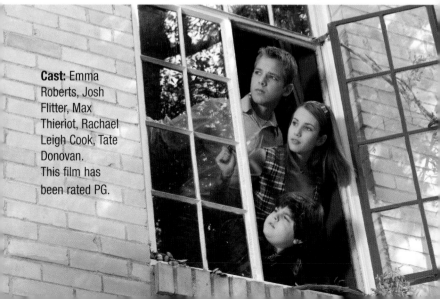

Cast: Emma Roberts, Josh Flitter, Max Thieriot, Rachael Leigh Cook, Tate Donovan.
This film has been rated PG.

Totally Spies!

Graphic Novel Episode Guide

Here's a groovy way to know what's in each Totally Spies graphic novel! Each book, available either in collectible hardcover or low-priced paperback editions, contains two complete full-color adventures starring your favorite teen Spies from Beverly Hills...

Totally Spies! Graphic Novel #1
"The O.P."

During a weekend road trip up the California coast, the girls' new car, a totally tricked-out, gadget-filled gift from Jerry to celebrate their recent success as super-spies, breaks down in a seemingly idyllic gated coastal town called Ocean Palisades – or "The O.P." for short. At first Alex, Sam, and Clover completely love it — the friendly, perfectly-tanned townspeople; the fancy, immaculate houses; the ridiculously scenic views – but, when they meet a few teens who seem to be too perfect to be real (they don't stay out after dark; they love spending time with their parents; they have sparkling teeth because they don't eat junk food), they start to get pretty weirded-out. Can the Spies find out what's really going on with the town's teens and save them from their crazy community – or will they be turned into perfect robot-like teens themselves and be forced to live in The O.P. forever?.

"Futureshock"

When the girls fiddle with Jerry's new time machine, they accidentally jet themselves 25 years into the future! At first they think it's way exciting – until they discover that Mandy is an all-powerful super villain who has control of all media! The spies are in awe when they see Mandy on the cover of every single magazine... starring in every single TV show and film... and dominating every single radio station – the whole time pushing her shallow Mandy agenda! And the worst part is, when the spies seek out their future selves, they discover that they're being held captive by Mandy! Desperate, present day Sam, Clover and Alex seek out future Jerry for help (he's the only one who knows how to work the time machine) — but to their shock, find that he's not exactly around anymore, he's had himself cryogenically frozen! The girls have to find a way to "thaw" him out, save the future versions of themselves from captivity, and stop Mandy before she totally "Mandifies" the planet!

Totally Spies!
Graphic Novel #2
"I Hate The 80s!"

Boogie Gus has updated his look a bit — unfortunately, not for the better. No longer a worshipper of the 70s, Gus has gleefully discovered the 80s. And he's bent on using his new device – "The Eightifier" to turn Beverly Hills into the ultimate 80s paradise. Can the Spies stop Boogie Gus before their home town goes retro for good? Can the girls deal with their complicated-to-maintain New Wave haircuts? Can they deal with all the synth-pop music at their school dances? Can they stop Jerry from wearing robin's egg blue sports jackets with the sleeves rolled up and pastel pink t-shirts underneath?!

"Attack Of The 50Ft. Tall Mandy!" It's time to crown the new Miss Beverly Hills. Among this year's hopeful contestants are Mandy and Clover. In order to get that extra winning edge, they both unwittingly decide to get a special full-body makeover that promises to make their hair, smiles, eyes and even their attitudes bigger. Mandy: "And everyone knows that bigger is better when it comes to this type of competition." But as they are getting their treatment, both strapped into separate full-body machines, a shadowy figure sneaks into the spa and puts a microchip into Mandy's machine. Mandy is suddenly growing bigger in every way. As the Spies start to investigate a rash of disappearances among Miss Beverly Hills contestants, they find out that Mandy, who has now grown nearly fifty feet tall, is behind the crimes. They also discover that along with becoming bigger physically, Mandy's meanness has also become magnified. And in an effort to win the competition, she decided to take out the other contestants. Can the Spies stop this monolithic Mandy menace before it's too late?

Totally Spies!
Graphic Novel #3
"Evil Jerry!"

Jerry's sinister brother Terence is at it again – and this time, with the help of Tim Scam, he's created a crazy device that has the ability to gather half of the evil from him... and transfer it directly into Jerry! Luckily, the spies start to notice that Jerry's acting strangely. And even luckier, they figure out what's going on – Terence and a troop of ex-villains are to blame! Yes, the girls finally discover the LAMOS! Can the spies save Jerry and WOOHP before it's too late – or will Terence proceed with the rest of his wicked plan – moving himself and the rest of the LAMOS out of their submarine and into WOOHP (from which they can spread their evil all over the world)?

"Deja Cruise!"

The spies are totally psyched when Jerry informs them that he's offering them a little vacation on the new WOOHP Cruise Liner – a state-of-the-art, luxury ship designed to be a pleasure boat for over-worked WOOHP agents! Once on the boat, the girls realize Jerry wasn't kidding, the ship is loaded with all sorts of amenities. Suddenly, the serenity of the vacation is broken as a gang of baddies, disguised as the ship's crew, take over the boat. Their plan: to destroy the ship with all of the WOOHP agents on it. The girls spring into action and try to defeat the villains, but their efforts only result in them accidentally causing the ship to sink. Or does it? The girls all wake up and find that things are back to normal. Was it all a bad dream caused by eating bad sushi? Suddenly, just as things seem to be back to normal, the entire incident happens again. The spies try to stop the villains, but again destroy the vessel. And yet, again, they wake up on the ship. The spies realize that they are re-living the same day over and over! And the only way to stop this vicious cycle is to defeat the bad guys. Can the girls figure out what to do, or will they be stuck on this boat forever?!

Totally Spies!
Graphic Novel #4
"Spies in Space"

The spies are way psyched when they find out that their favorite new band, The Alpha Centauris, are about to make music history. The band plans to be the first performers ever to broadcast a concert live from the moon. The only problem is, it's just days before the gig and the band is nowhere to be found. Apparently, their space transport has completely disappeared from WOOHP radar. Jerry puts the Spies on the case (as if they would have it any other way) and after GLADIS outfits them with cool intergalactic gadgets, including awesome space suits, the girls head off to find the band. After finding their abandoned ship, clues 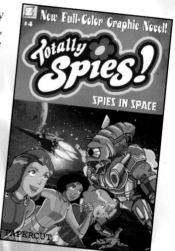 lead the Spies to believe the band was abducted by aliens. Can the girls save the band before they are evaporated by the sun?

"Spy Soccer"

It's the start of a new soccer season at Bev. High and Alex is psyched when her team gets a cool new coach. The only downside is that Clover and Sam feel a little snubbed because Alex is constantly busy with her team. Later, Jerry sends the girls on a mission to investigate a series of abductions. When the girls check out one of the crime scenes, they discover the place is totally trashed. And stranger still, one of the clues leads Sam and Clover back to… Alex?! When the girls confront Alex, she denies any wrongdoing, but can't explain or remember where she was at the time of the abduction. Then, seemingly out of nowhere, Alex's demeanor changes and she becomes very evil. She attacks Sam and Clover, and ultimately escapes. Sam and Clover discover that Alex's new soccer coach is using a special mind control ball to turn the Bev. High soccer team into her own private army – an army that uses their incredible, newfound, evil soccer techniques to get revenge on the coach's ex-teammates. Can Sam and Clover survive the final showdown – a death defying soccer match against the coach, Alex and her mind-controlled teammates?

The Hardy Boys in Comics
(and on TV and Vinyl)!

It's not that difficult to find an adult who remembers the late 70s live-action TV series, "The Hardy Boys Mysteries," with Shawn Cassidy and Parker Stevenson. And you can still find lots of Baby Boomers who recall the Hardy Boys serial, with Tim Considine and Tommy Kirk, which ran on the original Mickey Mouse Club TV series in the 50s. What's is almost impossible is finding anyone who might remember the Hardy Boys Saturday morning cartoon show from 1969. Like the Hardy Boys appearance on TV in the 50s, their animated TV series in the late 60s also inspired a four-issue comic-book series. But let's find out more about "The Mystery of The Forgotten Cartoon Series."

Back in the days long before entire cable networks were devoted to cartoons 24/7, the only place to see new cartoons on TV were on ABC, NBC, and CBS Saturday mornings. Back then Filmation Studios had a huge hit in the 60s with an animated series based on

the Archie comicbook characters. Not only was it a hit on TV, but the songs performed by the animated Archies band became huge pop music hits — and you thought Gorillaz was the first cartoon band! But the technology didn't yet exist that could make it possible for a "cartoon band" to per-

form live on tour. The producers at Filmation decided to try to launch another cartoon series, based on characters loved by millions of children, but this time, they'd also assemble a live band made up of singers and musicians that looked just like the cartoon characters.

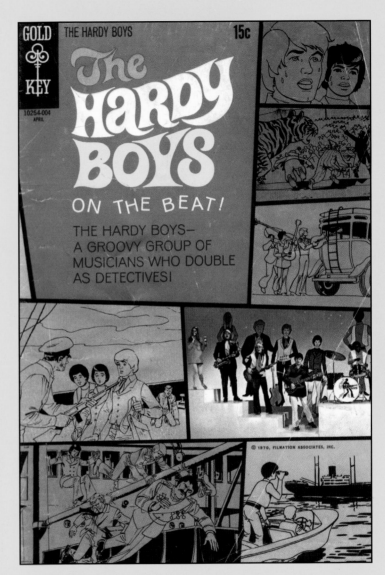

The Hardy Boys Gold Key Comicbook Checklist:
April 1970 – "Secret Of The Orinda Star," "The Dart-Riddle Rumble"
July 1970 – "Mystery Of The Catacombs," "Secret Mission"
October 1970 – "Mystery Of Wildcat Swamp," "The Headless Horseman"
January 1971 – "Paddle Wheel Peril" "The Guise Of Medusa"

The characters they chose to base this new show on was, of course, The Hardy Boys!

Filmation decided that in addition to solving mysteries, the Hardy Boys would be a touring bubblegum pop band. Joining Frank and Joe in this band, called The Hardy Boys Plus Three, were "Chubby" Morton, a character clearly based on Chet Morton, and new characters, Pete Jones (the first African-American character on a Saturday morning series*), and Wanda Kay Breckenridge.

For the non-singing parts of the show, actor Byron Kane provided the voices for Joe Hardy, Pete Jones, and Fenton Hardy; actor Dal McKennon did likewise for Frank Hardy and Chubby Morton, and

actress Jane Webb supplied the female voices for Wanda Kay Breckenridge and Aunt Gertrude Hardy.

While the actual mystery/adventure stories were animated, the show did feature the groovy live-action band briefly at the end of each episode performing one of their songs. Two record albums were released, "Here Come The Hardy Boys" and "Wheels," featuring the musical Hardy Boys, and the first album even cracked Billboard's Top 200 Album Chart. About the only other place to "see" the live version of The Hardy Boys Plus Three was on the Hardy Boys comicbook's covers. Each of the four covers featured a mix of comic art and photos. The "live" band appeared most prominently on the second issue.

Oh, and the answer to "The Mystery of the Forgotten Cartoon Series" is that the show ran against the ratings blockbuster Scooby-Doo and everyone was watching the Scooby gang!

*While the prime time TV special, "Hey, Hey, Hey, It's Fat Albert," debuted in 1969 as well, "Fat Albert and the Cosby Kids" didn't become a regular Saturday morning series until 1972. Like The Hardy Boys it was also produced by Filmation Studios.